Demon's Princess

By: Tiffany Keller

For more information address: tiffanykeller98@outlook.com This is a work of fiction. Names, characters, businesses, places, events, locales, and incidents are either the products of the author's imagination or used in a fictitious manner. Any resemblance to actual persons, living or dead, or actual events is purely coincidental.

Cover Design: Tiffany Keller

Editing: Tiffany Keller

Paperback IBSN: 979-8-3515906-1-5

Dedication

This is for all the women who wish a hot man on a motorcycle would come sweep you off your feet... Me too girl, me too.

<u>TRIGGER WARNING!!!!!</u>

This book contains multiple examples of (but not limited to):

- Rape
- Miscarriage
- Attempted Suicide
- Strong Language
- Alcohol Abuse
- Domestic Violence
- Sexual Assault
- Trauma
- Death
- Murder
- Violence
- Fire
- Kidnapping
- Mental Illness
- Pregnancy/Childbirth
- Scarification

And more. Please remember to practice self-care before, during, and after reading. Be sure you have access to self-comfort prior to starting this book if any of these topics are sensitive for you. Thank you for reading.

Tiffany Keller

Prologue

Remember to Breathe

Jo

Their voices carry into the kitchen where I am currently washing all the dishes left by the members from dinner. I know by the sound that it's my dad, the president of The Sinners Motorcycle Club, and my older brother, the Vice President.

"She shouldn't be allowed here. Not in our clubhouse," my brother says.

I slowly put the dish I was washing down into the sink to hear who they were talking about. Which one of the girls messed up this time?

"She won't be here in the morning when her buyer shows up. She can go be his new toy," my father says.

I know they sell women and I know it's wrong but as a woman in the MC world, you learn to shut up. In this world, a woman's word means absolutely nothing. Saying anything that goes against your President will only earn you a punishment.

I can't help but wonder who they are talking about as I slowly inch my way to the door, careful to step over the squeaky floorboards. I can't get caught listening to their private conversation or I will earn myself a punishment.

Just as I get close to the door that leads to the living room, it swings open hard, knocking me backwards off my feet. When I hit the floor, I hear the sickening cracking sound of my wrist breaking. I bite my lip to keep from crying out because I know that will just make this worse for me.

"Oh look, she started the party early," my brother sneers as he and my dad walk all the way into the kitchen. I have no idea why he's looking at me with such disgust in his eyes. I mean we've never been close since he had a different mother than I did but I don't remember doing anything to him to make him look at me that way.

As I attempt to pull myself off the kitchen floor, cradling my broken wrist, my brother, Artie, grabs me by the back of my hair painfully and says, "you no longer belong here cunt."

"What have I done?" I beg.

"You are no longer a part of this family. You are nothing but a whore, just like your mother was," my father spits at me angrily. What he's saying makes no sense to me. I thought he loved my mother all the way up until she died in a horrific car accident ten years ago.

I don't get a chance to ask what he means because Artie starts pulling on my hair, dragging me towards the door that leads to the basement cells.

I start thrashing as I beg, "Please, no, don't. I don't want to go down there. I haven't done anything to deserve a punishment, I swear."

"Stupid bitch. You'll do as you're told."

Artie drags me down the basement steps into the main room with my father following directly behind us. He turns me so my back is facing them and secures my wrists to the chains that hang from the ceiling. He raises me up until my legs no longer touch the floor and I know what comes next. There's no point in fighting the inevitable.

Artie pulls out his knife and proceeds to cut my shirt and pants from my body, leaving me in only my bra and panties. I feel cold air hit my back, sending a shiver down my spine. My head is wretched to the side, and I come face to face with the one man I thought would never sell me as a whore.

"Now you'll know what it's like to be treated as a whore," my father sneers.

As he lets go of my hair and takes a step back, I feel the first lashing of the whip. The searing pain of the fresh wound has me arching my back and screaming out loud. The next lashing comes harder than the first and I know Artie is playing his favorite game. The next eight lashes come the exact same way.

Suddenly, my arms are released from the shackles, and I fall directly onto my broken wrist, screaming out in pain. It sounds more like a croak since I spent so long screaming during the whipping. My head bounces off the concrete floor and my vision goes blurry.

I feel Artie's boot connect with my ribs and every breath is knocked out of my lungs. I roll over, trying to catch my breath when his boot connects with my ribs again. The third time, he kicks me so hard that my head hits the concrete again and my world turns black.

I don't know how long I stayed out but as I come to, I can hear my father and Artie talking slowly. They must think I'm still unconscious.

"Did you find out who spawned this bitch?" Artie asks.

"I knew her whore of a mother was cheating on me. It's the reason why I had her taken care of. The only thing I know is she was fucking some guy named Grizzly from the MC down in Sterling City," my father replies angrily.

I can't believe what I'm hearing. Not only is Bruce not my father but he had my mother killed. I see why she cheated on him considering he is the vilest man I have ever met but why would he kill her for that? I hold my tears in, so they don't realize I'm awake.

"Let's go find some pussy to bury ourselves in for the night. She's still passed out and should be that way for a while. We can come back in the morning to get her ready for Trent to retrieve his new property," my father, I mean Bruce, says laughingly.

As soon as I hear the basement door close, I open my eyes and start looking around for a way to escape this hell hole before I'm sold off to the worst man in the history of bad men. I've heard stories of the girls he buys that go missing, never to be heard from again.

I roll over until I can bear my weight on my good wrist and knees. I slowly use the wall to stand up. I'm barely able to breathe but I push through the pain so I can find my escape. I see the window next to the six barred cells is slightly cracked open. I roll my eyes at the two idiots. I get to the window and push it the rest of the way open. I punch my good fist into the screen until it pops out of the window frame.

I climb through the window until my feet touch the ground and then I begin walking as fast as I can. As I'm walking, I realize that the sticks and rocks stabbing into my bare feet are only a small price to pay for my freedom. I've lived here my entire life, so I know my way around. I may be only dressed in my bra and underwear, and I may have some serious injuries already, but I'll take that over what I just escaped from.

I walk as fast as my body can withstand until I finally make it to the road. I stay on the side, low into the ditch just in case they realize I'm missing and come find me. I start heading towards town so I can find some clothes and ride to Sterling City to start my search for my real father. He may not want anything to do with me, but I bet his MC is a lot more favorable that the one I just escaped from. It's more favorable than going with Trent.

I see headlights shining behind me and my heart starts beating faster because what if they found me already? I duck behind the tree closest to me, praying that whoever is driving didn't see me. I hear the car come to a stop and the door opens.

"Excuse me, miss, are you alright?" I hear a woman's voice ask.

I let out the breath that I was holding because they didn't find me, and I knew they would never send a woman to look for me. They don't trust women. I limp out from behind the tree and hear the girl gasp as she takes in the sight of my injuries and lack of clothing.

"Oh my god, what happened to you?" she asks.

"Please, I need a ride to town. I need to get some clothes and a ride out of this place," I say hoarsely.

"I'm not leaving you in town. I can give you a ride to wherever you need to go but I'm not about to drop you off anywhere close to this place with you looking like that," my rescuer says.

The girl, who looks to be around my age, rushes to me and helps me walk up the small ditch to her car. She helps me sit in the passenger seat and then rounds the car to get into the driver's seat. She reaches into the back seat and then hands me a blanket. I wince when the fabric touches my back, but I nod and smile at this woman.

"Thank you. I need to find the motorcycle club in Sterling City. My father is there, at least I think he is," I say as my adrenaline starts fading and so does my consciousness.

"Okay sweetie. Lie back and try to rest. Sterling City is about a four-hour drive. My name is Violet by the way," she says sweetly as she shifts the car into drive and heads down the road.

"Jo, and thank you again," I say as I start drifting off to sleep.

Chapter One

And Then We Met

Demon

I take a sip of my beer as I look at these fucking numbers again. I swear if I don't find a new Treasurer, I'm going to lose my mind trying to figure out the math that goes into keeping our books straight. I rub my eyes and glance at the clock, seeing that it's almost midnight. Damn, I must be getting old considering I'm dead tired. I close the accounting ledger and am about to leave my office when the phone starts ringing.

"What?" I bark at the prospect manning the front gate. I'm just ready to sleep.

"Pres, we have someone at the gate demanding to see you," he says quickly.

"The fuck? Who is it?" I demand.

"She said her name is Violet and she has something important to show you."

"Fuck, okay, I'm coming out there. Don't let her in the gate just yet," I say and hang up.

Who the fuck is Violet? And what the fuck would she need to show me at this house of night? I swear if it's another crazy ass ex of one of my men, I'm going to shove my foot so far up one of their asses.

I walk out of my office, making sure to lock the door. I make my way down the hallway and out the side door, avoiding the front room in case there's a brother in there. I don't need one of those nosy bastards asking questions I don't have the answers to.

As I approach the front gate, the prospect pushes the button to open it just far enough for me to walk out. I walk up to the blacked-out SUV and see a young girl with purple hair with a blank expression waiting for me.

"How can I help you darlin'?" I ask her.

"You can help me with the very injured girl currently passed out in my front seat," she replies coldly.

I try to look into her passenger seat to see if I know the girl she's talking about but all I can see is blonde hair and a blanket.

"And why would I help with that? This is a motorcycle club. The hospital is about 13 miles away. Take her there," I say and start walking back towards the front gate to go back inside.

"Well considering I picked her up in the Sinner's territory and she said her father was here, I figured I would bring her here to you," she replies.

My footsteps instantly halt and my blood boils at the mention of those nasty fuckers, the Sinners. They give motorcycle clubs a bad reputation since they deal in skins, or human trafficking.

"Sweetie, ain't no brother here old enough to have a child her age but I will take her in to see Doc before you leave," I say as I signal to the prospect to open the gates.

I wait for the girl to drive her cage through before walking in and shooting a text to Doc to meet me in the medic room. I walk to the passenger door and open it to retrieve the injured girl. As soon as I see her face, my heart starts beating faster. I have never in my 30 years seen such a beautiful woman. I instantly know that this girl is going to be mine.

I brush her blonde hair out of her face, and she stirs awake. Her bright blue eyes meet mine and it feels like everything clicks into place for me.

"Hey there Princess, my name is Demon," I say cautiously when I see the fear and panic in her eyes.

My girl shakes her head and tries to move away from me, causing her blanket to fall. I can't help but look down and what I see makes my blood boil with rage. My girl is covered in bruises, and I can see that her left wrist is hanging in a funny way meaning it's broken.

"Who the fuck did this to you?" I ask through gritted teeth.

She whimpers as she tries to scoot further away from me. I hold up both hands to show her I'm not a threat to her.

"Sweetie, this is the President of the motorcycle club you asked me to bring you to," Violet says. I shoot her an appreciative glance.

"My name is Jo. I'm looking for my father," my girl croaks out. Her voice is hoarse, but I don't see any marks on her neck, so she wasn't choked.

"Okay Princess, we can talk about that after you see Doc. I want him to look over your injuries and make sure you don't need to go to the hospital, okay?" I ask.

Jo looks at the other girl who nods slightly.

"Go ahead sweetie. I'll be right here," Violet says to my girl.

Jo looks at me with a softer expression and says, "I can't really walk by myself. I just need to lean on you to help."

"Okay Princess," I say as I grab her uninjured hand to help her step down out of the car. As soon as her feet hit the ground, she cries out and almost face plants the gravel. I immediately scoop her up and she cries out even louder. I feel liquid seep through the blanket on her back and I realize her injuries must be worse than I thought.

I look into her tearful eyes and say, "I'm sorry Princess. I'm going to walk as fast as I can to Doc and then I can set you down."

She nods her head and I take off walking as fast as I can, making sure the blanket stays covering her body.

If any of my guys see her body, I won't be held responsible for my actions.

Chapter Two

Counting Stitches

Jo

My back feels like it's on fire as Demon carries me into his clubhouse to the Doctor. As soon as I opened my eyes and saw Demon staring at me, I got scared. I had no idea where I was but as he and Violet explained that he was the President of the motorcycle club I was seeking, my fear deflated. I saw how handsome he was but I'm in no position to think about any man considering the one man I trusted caused all of this.

I cling to Demon's leather cut as he walks through the front door. As soon as we enter the main room, I see three guys in similar cuts drinking and sitting at one of the many tables in the room. They immediately get quiet when they see what or who Demon is carrying.

The biggest guy I have ever seen quickly stands up and drops his beer bottle which shatters on the floor. I look at his face and see my same blue eyes staring back at me. It's like looking in the mirror.

"Pres, w-what? Who is this?" the big guy asks.

"No time to explain. I gotta get her to Doc. I'll explain everything later after she gets checked out," Demon says, turning left down a hallway and walking faster than he was before.

"Who...?" I try to ask but the words get caught in my dry throat. That big guy looks so familiar. His eyes were just like mine. I wonder if he's related to me somehow or maybe he knows who my real father is.

Demon stops after passing two doors and stops outside a door with a red cross carved into the wood. He opens the door and as we walk in, I can see it's a makeshift hospital room complete with a hospital bed, cabinets full of medical supplies and an older man sitting on a stool in the corner.

When he notices Demon carrying me in, the older man jumps up from his stool and instructs Demon to lay me on the bed. As my back touches the bed, I let out a small painful whimper.

"Okay, let's roll her over onto her stomach so I can see what's going on with her back," the older man says to Demon.

They both gently push me onto my stomach, and I feel someone pull the blanket down off my back. Suddenly, there's a loud "FUCK" shouted and the sound of Demon's fist going through the wall. I try to turn to look at Demon and tell him I'm okay, but the older man says, "Pres, I've got this. Go get a drink and I'll come update you in a little bit."

I hear the door open and close, and I know Demon left. I'm kind of glad because I don't want to upset him.

"Girly, my name is Doc. These marks look deep, and some are going to need stitches. I know you have other injuries too, but I need to take care of these first, so they heal properly and don't become infected," Doc says.

"Okay," I whisper.

I hear him rustling through a cabinet and returning to my bedside. He puts his hand on my arm and I look up at him as he says, "I'm going to give you something that's going to make you go to sleep, so you won't feel a thing. I'll check your other injuries while you're out too."

"Okay," I whisper again as the tears threaten to drop down my cheeks.

"I hate to ask but I need to know. Were you sexually assaulted?" He asks gently.

"No. Just the lashes on my back, broken wrist and he kicked me in the ribs."

"Okay girly, let me get you that medicine. You'll feel a slight pinch and then you should start feeling sleepy quickly."

I feel a cold wet wipe my arm and then the pinch he told me about. After a few minutes, my eyes start to close, and I feel myself drift off. My only thought as I fall asleep is, I hope Demon is okay.

Chapter Three

Like Father, Like Daughter

Demon

I walk out of the hospital room so pissed and feeling the need to punch something else. I knew Jo's back was injured but I didn't expect to see at least ten whip marks bleeding everywhere. I start pacing the hallway as I think of ways to get revenge for my Princess. As I turn to make another pass down the hallway, Grizzly walks up to me and tries to speak but I cut him off before he can say anything.

"Not now, Grizzly."

"Yes, now. Who is that girl? And why does she look exactly like Brianna with my eyes?" he asks.

"Brianna? Your ex?" I ask, confused. He hasn't mentioned her in years. We haven't seen her in at least ten years.

"Yes. That girl in there looks exactly like a younger version of her but has my exact same eyes."

I stand still and think back to what Violet said when she brought Jo to the front gate. It all clicks into place, and I turn to Grizzly to deliver some crazy news.

"Brother, when Violet brought Jo here, she said she was looking for her father. I thought she was confusing our club with another one because I didn't think about the fact that our founder was old enough to be her father," I say.

"Jo… are you telling me there's a chance that girl in there is my daughter?" he asks sadly.

"I don't know for sure brother, but I will find out what she knows as soon as she's okay enough to talk," I tell him.

The door to the medic room opens and Doc walks out. The expression on his face tells me that I'm not going to like what he's about to say.

"What's the damage Doc?" I ask.

He glances sideways towards Grizzly, and I nod my head to signal that he's free to talk in front of Grizzly. I don't say anything about him possibly being Jo's father because that's not my business to tell.

"Well, she's got ten whips on her back and at least six were deep enough to require stitches. I gave her meds to put her to sleep, stitched her up and checked her other injuries," he says.

I swear I see red. I'm not sure how much more I can take hearing.

"What else?" I growl out.

"She has a broken wrist that I reset and put in a splint. She has some bruised ribs which should heal on their own. She also has a lot of scars. I'm not sure what she's been through but she's strong enough to have endured all of whatever caused all those scars," he says regretfully.

"Are you fucking kidding me? Who the fuck would do that to her?" Grizzly explodes.

I clench my jaw and fists because I'm on the verge of storming the Sinner's territory and killing every single one of them. I know they are the ones responsible for my Princess laying in that hospital bed. Fuckers.

"Sinners," I say through clenched teeth.

"You're shitting me Pres. What would a girl like that be doing with the Sinners?" Doc asks.

I shake my head and say, "I don't know but I plan on finding out as soon as she wakes up and can talk to me."

"She'll be asleep for a while and I think we should keep her that way for a couple of days to give her body a chance to recuperate," Doc says.

"Fine, but we move her to my room. I want to be able to keep an eye on her," I say.

"I'll move her for you Pres," Grizzly volunteers and walks into the medic room leaving me in the hallway with Doc.

"Look, I'm not disrespecting you or your choices, but I think you need to be careful. We don't know why she was coming here or if the Sinners sent her here on purpose," Doc says.

I narrow my eyes at him and say, "Don't tell me how to run my club Doc. I know why she's here and you should be able to trust my judgment as your President."

He holds up his hands and nods his head at me. Doc walks off as Grizzly comes out with Jo cradled in his arms. Not going to lie, a twinge of jealousy courses through me. I don't want any other male touching my girl, but I just shake those feelings off. Grizzly walks further down the dimly lit hallway, stopping just outside of my door. I follow behind and pull out my keys to unlock the door. I gesture for Grizzly to go inside, and he obliges. He walks to the bed and sets my Princess down on her side.

"She looks so much like Brianna. If she is my daughter, I want a chance to get to know her," Grizzly whispers. I nod my head at him before he walks out of my room. I pull my recliner up right next to the side of the bed. I grab Jo's hand and hold it as I promise to protect her with my life. I lay my head down on top of our clasped hands and close my eyes.

I finally drift off to sleep, dreaming of my future with my Princess.

Chapter Four

Everyone Has a Story…

Jo

I slowly blink my eyes open and immediately close them again when the harsh sunlight reaches them. After a few minutes, I slowly blink my eyes open again and look around the unfamiliar bedroom I am currently in. There's not much in here, just the bed I'm lying in, a dresser directly in front of me and a giant TV attached to the wall above the dresser. I swing my eyes to the right when I hear a snoring sound and find Demon asleep in a recliner that was pulled next to it.

I take my time looking at him since I didn't get much of a chance when I first got to the clubhouse. He has black hair that's shorter on the sides but longer on the top and a square jawline that has the beginnings of a beard growing on it. He's sleeping with his legs propped up on the edge of the bed and his arms crossed but his muscles fill out his shirt completely. He looks one deep breath away from shredding his gray t-shirt to pieces. He is absolutely the most handsome man I have ever met, and my heart skips a beat when I take in all of him. But I know to be cautious of the President of a motorcycle club considering I'm in this condition because of one.

I notice my body feels stiff, so I try to readjust myself causing a blinding pain to shoot across my back. I let out a small whimper of pain and Demon's eyes snap open. His bright green eyes meet mine and I see his expression harden.

"Where are you going Princess?" his deep voice filters into my ear, rough from sleep.

"I was just trying to adjust myself because it feels like I've been laying in the same position for weeks. But I think it's a better idea to just lay here," I whisper, looking away from him. Looking directly into the eyes of the President is seen as a challenge.

"You've been out for about two days. I was waiting for you to wake up."

"Am I okay?" I ask.

"Yes. Doc stitched you up and reset your wrist. Your ribs will heal on their own," he answers as he leans forward, resting his elbows on his knees. I can see him out of the corner of my eyes, but I keep my eyes focused on the dresser.

"Princess, look at me," he commands softly.

I swing my gaze to his and I see his expression soften.

"What happened to you? You came into my club with injuries that would make a grown man cry," he asks gently. I don't want to tell him the gritty details but when the President asks you a question, you answer it honestly or risk facing punishment.

"Where should I start?" I huff out, swinging my gaze to the ceiling. I won't be able to look at him while I explain.

"The beginning. Who did this to you and why?"

I pause and take a deep breath, but it sends more pain through my chest. I take a minute to gather the courage to tell him everything.

"My father and brother did this to me," I say quietly.

"WHAT?" he roars, and I flinch at his outburst, but I don't think he notices as he jumps up from the chair and begins pacing the floor from the door to the wall and back. The tears well up in my eyes but I don't let them fall. First rule, never show any weakness even if a punishment is inevitable.

I keep going before he can try to say anything else. Once I open the gates, everything comes flooding out.

"I was in the kitchen washing dishes when I overheard my father, well Bruce, and Artie talking about how some girl doesn't belong in the clubhouse anymore. I know it was wrong to listen in but I just wanted to know which one of the girls had screwed up so I tried to walk closer to the door to see if I could hear better. As soon as I got to the door, it swung open, knocking me down. That's how I broke my wrist. Artie came into the kitchen and grabbed me by the hair saying I was the one who didn't belong anymore. Him and Bruce dragged me down to the punishment cells in the basement. They whipped me to show me how a whore was treated. After that, my chains were released, and Artie kicked me until I passed out. When I came to, I heard them talking about how my mom cheated on Bruce with someone named Grizzly in the motorcycle club in Sterling City. Apparently, he's my real father. I let them think I was still passed out and heard them say Trent was coming to buy me in the morning," I rushed out.

"How did you escape?" Demon growls.

I let out a small laugh, which also hurts. "Those idiots left the window cracked and I escaped through it. I ran until I got to the road and that's where Violet picked me up. I told her to bring me here to find my real father."

"And who are Bruce and Artie to the Sinners MC? You came from their territory," he asks.

I swing my eyes to his stormy ones and say, "They are the President and Vice President of the Sinner MC."

Chapter Five

Past is Experience

Demon

I am holding on by a thread as Jo explains that her piece of shit father and brother are the ones who hurt her and were planning on selling her to Trent.

"Princess, I know this is a lot to talk about, but I have one more important question. Why are you covered in scars?"

She lets out a long breath and looks like she really doesn't want to explain but I need to know. It's selfish but I have to know exactly what happened to her so I can get the proper revenge on those fuckers. They are going to learn firsthand why they call me Demon.

"They called them punishments. Us women were given a list of rules and if we didn't follow them, they would punish us with some form of violence. They said that's how the motorcycle club world works," she says.

I immediately start shaking my head and say, "No. They lied. That's how those sick fuckers worked. We don't do anything like that here."

I can see she doesn't believe me, but she will see it for herself as she spends more time here. We believe that women and children deserve the most respect considering we wouldn't have shit without them. I change the subject before I completely lose my shit.

"So, they said Grizzly was your real father? What's your mother's name?"

"Brianna Weeks," she says, eying me curiously.

"Okay, that makes sense now. Grizzly talked to me and said you two have the same eyes or some shit like that. He wants to meet you. Would you be up for that?" I ask her carefully.

"Yes, please," she begs. I knew she was strong, but I swear this girl is indestructible. You would think that after everything she went through, she wouldn't want to meet another guy who could be her father that's also part of a motorcycle club but of course, Jo does.

"Okay, Princess. I'll tell him to come in and then I'll go get you some food and get Doc to come check you out."

"Come in?" she asks, confused.

I let out a little chuckle and said, "Yeah, he's been camped out in the hallway waiting for you to wake up so he could talk to you."

"Really? Why?" she asks.

"He said if his daughter is hurt, he's going to be there for her when she wakes up," I say.

A small smile tilts her lips, and she nods her head. I stood back up from the recliner that I had sat back down in as Jo explained the rest of her story. I stretch my arms over my head. Sleeping in this chair for two days has been killing my muscles. I catch Jo staring at me, so I throw her a wink as I head to the door to unlock it. I throw it open and see Grizzly passed out, snoring like the bear he is so I kick his boot, startling him awake.

"Grizz, she wants to meet you. I'm going to get her some food and get Doc to check her out. Give you two a chance to talk," I say as I walk out of my room.

Grizzly shoots up off the floor and nods his head. He walks into my room and closes the door. I want to give them some time together because I know this won't be easy for either of them. I turn to go get my Princess some food as she gets to know her real father.

Chapter Six

Meeting The Father

Jo

I watch as the giant man that dropped his beer bottle in front of me, walks through the bedroom door that Demon just walked out of. I look to see if I can spot any resemblance to me. He's a huge man but not in a fat way, just built with a lot of muscles. He has brown hair that is cut close to his head and bright blue eyes just like mine.

Grizzly walks over to Demon's abandoned recliner and takes a seat. Looking around, he wrings his hands in his lap for a few minutes before finally saying "Sorry. You just look so much like your mom."

I feel the tears well up in my eyes because I miss my mom so much. I feel horrible if Bruce was telling the truth and was the one to take her away from not only me but Grizzly as well. I can see the love he had for her shining in his eyes.

"Thank you. I miss her," I say.

"Is she okay? Does she know you are okay?" He asks. He doesn't know.

"Oh… um… She died ten years ago. Car accident," I say regretfully.

"What?" Grizzly whispers. I can see his heart breaking. He must have really loved my mom.

"Yeah… well at least that's what I was told but Bruce said he had her taken care of because he found out she had been with you. I'm not sure what the truth is but I feel like you should know," I say.

I watch as Grizzly's face morphs from sadness to anger. He has a vein in his forehead that has popped out now and looks as if it's going to burst at any moment. His face turns a nice shade of red and I can see his jaw clenching shut. He closes his eyes and takes a deep breath to calm himself before speaking.

"I'll have one of my brothers investigate what really happened with your mom. In the meantime, I would really like to get to know you, if you're okay with that?" he asks.

"Don't you want to get a DNA test done or something?" I ask skeptically. He has no proof that I'm his daughter so I wouldn't be offended if he wanted to get one done. I tell him just as much, but he just shakes his head and lets out a small laugh.

"We can get one done if it will help you, but I can already tell you that you are my daughter."

I don't want to contradict what he says so I just nod my head and smile at him.

"Okay. Enough of all of that. Tell me everything about yourself. Tell me anything you think I should know about you," he says excitedly.

We proceeded to talk for a long while, me telling him about growing up with the Sinners, my mom, my dreams to go to college and so much more. Grizzly tells me about how he came to be part of the Blue Devils to escape the trailer park he was growing up in. He tells me about his memories of my mom, which causes me to cry happy tears. I haven't heard stories about her in so long because once she died, Bruce refused to talk about her. I thought it was his grief but now I know it's probably because he killed her.

We talk for so long that the sun starts setting when Demon returns with Doc in tow. Grizzly excuses himself and tells me he will be right down the hall if I need anything. He kisses my forehead and says goodbye. I have to turn my attention to Demon and Doc to keep myself from crying. I haven't felt this loved in so long, since my mom was alive.

"Hey girly, are you ready for me to check you over?" Doc asks as he sits down on the edge of the bed. I nod my head as he lifts my shirt up to look at my bruised ribs. After poking me a few times, causing me to whimper, Demon tells him he's done. Doc hands me some pain medication as he explains that I'll be sore for a couple of weeks, but I should heal completely.

I thank him and take the pills, laying back down. Demon takes his place in the chair next to the bed. My eyes start to drift closed, and I feel Demon grab my hand, holding it between his. I fell asleep with a smile on my face and my brain filled with images of Demon.

Chapter Seven

Revenge Will Be Sweet

Demon

I watch my Princess fall asleep with a smile on her face. I think meeting Grizzly today really helped her with being in our clubhouse. Speaking of her being here, I take my phone out of my pocket and send a group text to the guys, calling for Church in ten minutes. It's time to tell them about Jo and to make plans for revenge on those pieces of shits.

I stand up from the recliner and regretfully release Jo's hand. I tuck the covers around her before heading out and making my way down the hall. I stop outside of the double doors that lead to the meeting room and take a deep breath. I can hear my brothers talking behind the door, so I push them open and make my way to my chair sitting at the head of the table.

This room is meant for Church, meetings our club has about important shit. There's a giant wooden table with our emblem carved in the middle, a skull lit on fire with blue flames. There are eleven chairs surrounding the table, reserved for the officers and members of the club that I trust to be in these meetings. We don't allow prospects or women in this room. There are ten of my brothers surrounding the table, waiting to hear why I called an emergency meeting.

My eyes meet with Grizzly's across the table, and I give him a subtle nod to tell the men about Jo. Normally I would have said something but since I haven't officially claimed Jo, I'll let her father be the one to tell the brothers.

"Alright, fuckers. My daughter has shown up here, beaten and abused for years. Her name is Jo. Her mother was my old lady from ten years ago, Brianna," Grizzly grunts out.

I look around and watch the looks of shock on all of my guys' faces. Jaws hand open and the room has gone completely silent. You could hear a feather drop in here.

Rooster is the first to say something.

"You're fucking with us, right?" my Treasurer asks.

"No, I'm not fucking with you. She came here after her piece of shit brother and the guy claiming to be her father beat the fuck out of her," Grizzly growls.

"How are you sure she's telling the truth and wasn't just sent here with a sob story?" my tech guy, Brick, asks.

It's a valid question but hearing anyone talk bad about my Princess sets me on edge, so I finally speak up.

"We saw the injuries she has and had. I personally talked to her, and I trust what she is saying is the truth."

All my brothers nod their heads. They know to trust my judgment. It's why I'm the President.

"Jo will be with us for the foreseeable future. She will be treated like a Princess. No exceptions. Also, she is off limits to everyone in here," I say.

Brute, my Vice President, gives me an incredulous look like I've lost my mind, but I just ignore him. I don't have to tell anyone shit about my decisions. Jo is mine but she isn't ready for that yet so I'm just going to declare her off limits to my brothers.

"Right, so all you fuckers keep your hands to yourself," Grizzly agrees with me. Little does he know I plan to claim Jo as soon as she is ready.

"So, what happened to her exactly?" Brute asks.

I started explaining everything that Jo had told me with Grizzly adding in anything extra she had told him. I tell my guys how she showed up here and what Doc had said happened. By the time we finish explaining, I can feel the rage radiating off every man in the room.

"So, we are getting revenge, right?" my enforcer, Viper, asks. Crazy fucker is always looking for an opportunity to use his special knives.

"Yes, we are but I called this meeting to figure out the best way to get our revenge on those nasty fuckers. I want to send a message that no one fucks with a Blue Devil," I say.

"I say we do some recon on them and then come up with a plan to take all of them out in one swoop," Trigger, my Sergeant at Arms, contributes.

"I like that idea, but the President and Vice President are to be brought back here and into the basement," I growl.

"I know it's normally not our way to involve women in our plans but maybe we should let Jo decide what happens to those two," Grizzly grunts. I immediately shake my head no.

"No, I don't want her anywhere near them again. She's been through enough already because of those assholes," I spit, venomously.

"Exactly, Pres. Think about it. She was put through hell at their hands. Don't you think she should be allowed to at least be considered in deciding what happens to those fuckers? She's stronger than you are giving her credit for," Grizzly says.

I think it over for a minute and say, "Fine, I'll talk to her about it after she gets some rest but no guarantees. Brick, see if you can get us eyes into the Sinner's territory and clubhouse. Take Ghost if you need his help getting in. Also, investigate the accident involving Brianna. Jo said Bruce admitted to killing her. I want to know if it's true. We will all meet again on this subject in a few days. Anything else anyone has to add?" I ask.

All my brothers shake their heads no so I bang my gavel on the table, signaling the end of Church. All the brothers file out of the room and head towards the main room to get a drink from the bar. I head in the opposite direction, towards my room where my Princess is waiting for me.

Chapter Eight

Every Day Brings New Choices

Jo

I slowly blink my eyes open and notice I am still in Demon's bed. I feel his hand holding mine, so I swing my gaze towards him and find him watching me. His hair is wet, and he's only dressed in a pair of dark blue sweatpants. My mouth waters at the sight of his ripped abs and arms that are covered in tattoos. My eyes travel back to his face, and I start to blush as I realize he caught me checking him out. I avert my gaze to the ceiling as he releases a chuckle.

"It's okay, Princess. You can look anytime you want," he says.

I release a small laugh and change the subject. "So, what's up? You look like you need to tell me something."

"I do. I told my brothers about you at Church last night. I had to tell them what happened to you so they would know why I wanted to take revenge against the Sinners," he says quietly.

I'm not mad. I understand why he had to tell his men. I tell him just that and he looks relieved.

"Okay. So, we talked about how we wanted to get our revenge on the Sinners. Normally, we don't allow women to get involved in any kind of plans like this because we want to keep them safe. But since they are the ones who hurt you, I told Grizzly that I would ask you what you wanted to happen to Bruce and Artie," Demon says.

I sit and think for a few minutes. I think about all the whips, the punches, the slaps and every other injury they have ever caused me, and it helps me make my decision.

"I want to be the one to hurt them. I want to be the one they see getting revenge," I say.

Demon shakes his head no and says, "I don't want you anywhere near them. I want to keep you safe. You can decide what happens to them but me and Grizzly will be the ones to carry out your decision."

I shake my head no before he even finishes his sentence. "I know I'm not supposed to challenge anything you say but I can't let what they did to me my entire life go. I need this, Demon. I need to be the one to hurt them like they hurt me so many times. Please," I beg.

"First, you call me Derrick. If it's just us, my name is Derrick to you. Second, if it's just us, you can talk to me about anything. Your safety is my priority so I may make decisions you don't like but you can always discuss things with me. That doesn't mean you are challenging me. I'm not like those dirty fuckers who want to control your every move, Princess," Demon, I mean Derrick, says.

"Thank you for saying all of that. I just need to be the one to hurt them like they hurt me Derrick, I hope you understand that."

Derrick thinks about what I said for a few minutes before saying, "Okay. Here's my compromise. We will be the ones to take out the rest of the Sinners and we will bring Bruce and Artie back here for you to get your own revenge."

"Thank you, Derrick," I say.

"Don't thank me yet. The only way I'm letting you do this is if you train with me so I know you can handle it if anything happens," he says.

"Okay, I'm fine with that. I've always wanted to train just in case any of the guys wanted to try something worse than just knocking me around," I say.

"No one will ever lay a hand on you in violence ever again if I have anything to say about it. Now, you need to rest up because as soon as you're healed enough, training begins," Derrick commands.

I giggle and ask him if I can finally get a shower. I've been laying in this bed for days and I feel disgusting. I can only imagine what I look like.

"Of course, Princess. Do you think you can do it by yourself, or do you need some help?" He asks.

"I'll probably need help getting out of the bed and getting to the bathroom, but I should be able to shower myself," I say.

"How about a bath instead? I don't want to risk you falling in the shower," he argues.

"That'll work. I just want to clean myself."

Derrick gets up and heads to the door on my left. He walks into the bathroom, and I hear him turn the water on to fill up the bathtub. He comes back and puts one arm under my shoulders and the other under my knees. He lifts me to his arms causing me to squeal and throw my arms around his neck, holding on for dear life. He chuckles and carries me into the bathroom.

Derrick sits me on the counter next to the sink and goes to turn the water off since the tub is filled. I see that he added bubbles and I get excited to finally be able to get clean and smell better.

"Okay, arms up Princess," Derrick says as he walks back over to me and lifts my shirt over my head. I'm not wearing a bra since I have stitches in my back so when Derrick takes my shirt off, his eyes immediately dart down to my naked breasts. I can tell he is trying to ignore them, and it makes me release a giggle.

"Princess, you're hurt. I'm trying my best to help you but you're not making this easy," he groans.

My body heats as Derrick proceeds to take my panties off so I'm sitting in front of him completely naked. He picks me up and sets me down in the bathtub. I groan as the warm water reaches my skin.

"Okay, I'm going to get you some clothes. You just relax and I'll come get you when you are done," he says as he practically sprints out the bathroom door.

.....

After my bath, I make my way back into Derrick's bedroom and see him standing there looking so handsome.

"I figured you were tired of lying in this room. Do you want to go tour the clubhouse?" he asks, bringing my attention back to his face.

"Sure," I reply.

Derrick loops his arm around my waist as he opens his bedroom door and leads me into a hallway. I look to my right and see a lot of doors, all closed.

"Those are the officers of the club's rooms. We aren't required to live here but none of us have an Old Lady, so we all stay here," Derrick explains.

We turn to the left and walk until the hallway opens into a massive bar room. There is a bar on the far right with at least ten bar stools filled with members of the motorcycle club. There are booths that line the wall to the left, tables with chairs scattered all around the room and pool tables set up to play a game. I quickly divert my attention to the pictures on the walls. There are hundreds of pictures of the members of the Blue Devils, old and new.

As I am looking at everything on the walls, I come across a poster with a list of their club rules on it. It reads:

1. We protect our brothers with our lives

2. Members must ride a bike (NO EXCEPTIONS)

3. All Church meetings are MANDATORY!!!!! (If you miss a meeting, you better have a damn good reason)

4. You must wear your colors/cut at all times! (Unless you are in the bedroom)

5. Loyalty to the club is a priority. If you can't be loyal, find another club

6. Women and Children are treated like royalty! If it wasn't for them, we would have no purpose in this life.

7. What is said and done in the club, STAYS IN THE CLUB!!!!!!

8. No hard drugs. Weed is fine.

9. Prospects will prospect for at least six months unless the President overrides

10. Prospects must do anything a patched member tells him to do with no complaints

After reading the rules, I realize that these guys are nothing like the Sinners, sending a wave of relief through my body. Derrick stays by my side as I look at everything plastered to the walls. Eventually we make our way to the bar and Derrick starts introducing everyone.

"I am going to go down the line. We have Brute, Trigger, Axle, Rooster, Viper, Brick, Gearhead, Ghost, and Ink. Prospects are behind the bar and manning the front gate. We have five prospects total right now," Derrick explains.

"We may not be big, but we still get the job done," Rooster says as he winks at me. I laugh at his inuendo.

"Alright, Rooster. That's enough," Derrick growls. I lean into his side, and he smiles down at me.

"Where is Grizzly?" I ask.

"Out on a run for me. Speaking of, Rooster, I need to talk to you in my office later," Derrick says in his direction.

"Got it, Pres," Rooster replies.

After talking to the guys for a while and getting something to eat from the kitchen, we make our way back to Derrick's room when I start yawning. He helps me lay back down in the bed and covers me up.

"Okay, Princess. Get some rest. We start training in a week," he announces at I start to drift off to sleep.

Chapter 9

2 Months Later

Demon

I swing my fist towards Jo's face, and she blocks it perfectly. I go to congratulate her, but she slips her foot behind mine and takes me to the ground, knocking the wind out of me. I hear a loud booming laugh and look up to see Grizzly hunched over, holding his stomach laughing at me. I give him the finger as I stand back up.

"Sorry, I got excited and caught up in the moment," Jo says sheepishly.

"Don't apologize, good job. Brute, come spar with Jo," I yell as I make my way to Grizzly.

"Man, she really knocked you on your ass," he laughs.

"Ha. Ha. She's doing really well. I think she's ready," I say as I watch Jo take down Brute. A smile tilts my lips because Brute is a big fucker, and she took him down like it was nothing.

"I see the way you look at her, Pres. Are you planning on claiming my little girl?" Grizzly asks, surprising the fuck out of me. I thought I hid my feelings better than that.

"If she lets me, yeah I do," I say. No point in beating around the bush if he's already figured it out.

Grizzly's face turns serious as he says, "Oh, she will. I see the way she looks at you too. But know this, I just got her in my life so if you hurt her, President or not, I will kill you myself."

I throw my hands up in front of me and say, "You don't have to worry about that Grizz. I would never hurt her. She's going to be my Old Lady."

"Good. If I could have chosen any of the brothers for her to end up with, it would be you."

"Thanks man. So, is that all you needed?" I ask, impatiently wanting to get back to Jo. We have grown close over the past two months as we trained together almost every day.

"No. We've been watching the Sinners and they look like they are having some trouble with our boy Trent. Someone set their garage on fire," he laughs but I don't join in.

"The only reason Trent would be pissed is if he's still looking for Jo," I say angrily.

"Don't worry, Demon. He won't find her here. No one knows where she went. We've listened to Bruce and Artie. They always come up with the dumbest places to look for her."

"Okay. You're probably right. I just don't like the fact that he's looking so hard for her," I say.

"Me either but she's safe here. Now, everyone wants to know if the party is still happening later?" Grizzly asks.

I look at him like he's stupid and say, "Yeah. It's a celebration for Jo. After all she's been through, she deserves to celebrate her recovery. She's made one hell of a comeback."

"Very true. Alright, I'm heading to the store to get the food for later. Holler if you need anything else," he says as he walks off.

I walk back over to Jo and Brute, who are taking a drink of water.

"Hey Princess. That's enough training for today. We have two hours until the party so go get ready," I tell Jo.

"Okay. Where are you going?" she asks innocently.

"I have some club business to take care of before the party."

Jo nods once at me and takes off walking towards the clubhouse. I can't help but admire her sweet ass as she walks away. I swear she knows I'm watching because she adds a little sway to her walk, causing my mouth to water. I hear a chuckle next to me and turn to see Brute holding in his laughter.

"Shut the fuck up, Brute. Not a word," I growl.

He throws his hands up in front of him and says, "Pres, you are so screwed."

"Don't I know it," I sigh.

"Let's go handle this club business so we can get to the party," Brute says as he starts walking towards the back door. I shake my head and follow behind him, my mind drifting back to my Princess. Tonight, I'm claiming her as mine.

Chapter Ten

Party Foul

Jo

I look around at all the people who came to celebrate my recovery and I realize that this is what family is supposed to be like. All the Blue Devils are scattered around the backyard of the clubhouse. Ink, Gearhead, and Viper are standing by the fire sipping on beers as three club girls try to get their attention. I laugh and roll my eyes at the lack of attention they are showing the girls. I swing my gaze to the left and see Rooster, the goofball, attempting to balance a beer can in between Trixie's breasts but ultimately failing. I laugh as his beer drops to the ground and an adorable pout takes over his face.

"Having fun, Princess?" My body shudders as Derrick's voice penetrates my ears. I turn around to face him.

"Of course. Are you?" I raise my eyebrow as I ask him. A genuine smile spreads over his face and it nearly takes my breath away. This man has no idea how much he affects me.

"I am now," he winks, and I swear I almost melt into a puddle. I tried to keep my distance from Derrick but after two days, I gave up. We trained together every single day so I knew ignoring these feelings I have for him wouldn't work. I've been waiting for him to make a move, but he hasn't. I really hope what I'm feeling isn't one sided.

"Is that so? Well, let's have some more fun," I say as I grab his hand, sending an electric shock up my arm. I pulled him over to the table we had set up to play some kind of flip cup game. The club girls thought of it so we would have something else to do besides standing around drinking.

"Let's play," I say to Derrick.

He shakes his head and pulls on my hand that's still wrapping in his. "Princess, I don't want to play some high school frat party game. I just want to spend time with you," he says as he wraps his arms around me. I melt into his arms and wrap my arms around his waist, propping my chin on his chest, looking into his eyes.

"Okay, Derrick."

Derrick moves one hand to the back of my head, cradling it and his other hand goes to my hip. He leans his face down, searching for any resistance I might give him, but he won't find any. I've wanted him to kiss me every day for the past two months.

Just as our lips touch, it feels like fireworks explode in my head. IT takes me a minute to realize what is happening. Everything happens in slow motion. One second, I'm finally having my first kiss with Derrick and the next, I'm being tackled to the ground with Derrick laying on top of me, gunfire exploding around us.

"Derrick, what's happening?" I ask, my voice trembling.

"The front gate was blown open. I need to go help my brothers. Stay here until I get back," he commands.

I nod my head and then give him a chaste kiss and say, "Be safe."

"Always." He pulls his gun out of his holster and takes off running in the direction of the gunfire. I hunker down behind the tree that I was tackled next to and wait. A few minutes later, the gunfire suddenly stops, and I hope that means this is over. I peek my head around the tree to see if I can spot Derrick but what I see is even worse than anything I could have ever imagined.

Standing in the middle of the backyard is Trent's second in command, Ryan, with his gun pressed to the back of Derrick's head.

Chapter Eleven

Risking it All

Demon

This can't be fucking happening. One second, I'm finally kissing my Princess and the next, our front gate was blown apart by a bomb and easily 100 men with semi-automatics storm inside. My men took out a couple of their men in monkey suits but there weren't enough of us. As I stand here with some dumbasses gun pressed to the back of my head, I pray that Jo listens to me and stays put.

"What do you want?" I growl loud enough so this guy can hear me. I look around and notice every one of my men and club girls have a gun pressed to the back of their heads too.

"I'm here for a girl. Sweet little thing named Jo," the smug fucker says.

I grit my teeth and my hand curls into fists as I ask, "Why?"

"Because the boss man paid a pretty penny for her and he wants his property back," He laughs.

"Tough shit for Trent. She's not here," I say, trying to buy me some time to figure out a way out of this mess.

The guy behind me clicks his tongue and says, “Now, now. I don’t like liars.”

Suddenly, one of his guys pulls the trigger and I watch as Trixie falls to the ground, lifeless. All my men look away from the scene. There’s blood everywhere and a huge gaping hole in the back of her head. I know she was a club girl, but she was under our protection and didn’t deserve to die because of me.

“I’ll ask again. Where is Jo?” he asks. I shake my head but don’t say a word.

“Okay, have it your way. Guys, bring all the sluts up here,” he commands. One by one, all my club girls, Old Ladies, and even Violet, are kneeled in front of me. Each one has a man pressing a gun to the back of their skull.

“I’m going to ask you where Jo is and every time you lie or don’t answer, my men will put a bullet in the head of a woman here,” the sick bastard says, sounding excited.

I’m stuck between a rock and a hard place. I don’t want any of these women to die but I can’t just give Jo to these sick bastards.

“Now, where is my boss’ property?”

I look around at my men and see the pity in their eyes. They know how hard this decision is for me. Suddenly, the guy standing behind Violet cocks his gun and that sets off Viper. He starts yelling, “YOU FUCKING DICK. If you touch her, I will hunt you down and kill you painfully.”

I see the tears in Violet’s eyes as she nods to me. She knows I can’t give up Jo’s location and is prepared to die to protect her friend.

"STOP," I hear yelled from the tree line. I start shaking my head and yelling at JO to stay away. She, of course, doesn't listen and walks out of the forest, straight up to the idiot holding a gun to my head. I try to get her attention, but she avoids looking at me. My heart sinks in my chest because I'm pretty sure I know what she's doing.

"Ryan, I'll go with you. But you have to let Violet and everyone else go," Jo says.

My heart drops to my stomach. I try to tell her no but as soon as I open my mouth, Ryan brings the butt of his gun down on my skull and I fall to my knees. Jo grabs Ryan's arm as he raises it to hit me again.

"Ryan, no, please just stop. I'll go with you, please," she begs.

"Very well. Come on. The boss has been waiting impatiently," Ryan says as his men start walking towards the gate. I try to make a move to grab Jo but Ryan hits me across the face with his gun again. He grabs Jo, putting her back to his front and his gun to her temple.

"Try anything like that again, and I'll blow her head off."

A growl escapes my lips, but I see the fear in Jo's eyes when her eyes finally reach mine.

I'm sorry, she mouths

I'll come for you, I promise, I mouth back.

"Oh, and Jude, grab the purple haired bitch too. I want her for myself," Ryan says excitedly. The guy, Jude, grabs Violet and shoves her forward. Viper lets out a loud growl and attempts to move towards Violet.

"Ah, Ah, Ah. I'll shoot her faster than you can blink. Get back biker boy," Jude says as he digs his gun into Violet's temple.

"I'll come find you, Princess. I promise." I say to Jo. She nods her head, but I can see the doubt floating behind her eyes. Ryan leads Jo out of the front gate, Jude and Violet following. They get into a gray SUV and take off.

All at once, Viper screams "FUCK" and I throw a lawn chair across the lawn. It breaks as it hits a tree. I look around at my brothers and I know they are just as eager to get Jo back. I nod my head and yell "CHURCH. NOW."

I stop on my way in and realize there's still a dead Trixie laying in the grass. Rooster is sitting next to her on the grass, holding her hand. "Prospects, clean up out here. Doc, will you take care of Trixie?" I command.

"Got it, Pres," Doc says.

We all file into the meeting room we use for Church and start talking about a game plan to get our girls back.

I'm coming, Princess.

Chapter 12

Destination: Hell

Jo

Violet and I are thrown into the back of a gray SUV by Ryan's goon, Jude. I land hard on my shoulder as Violet lands on her back. I hear her suck in a breath and I immediately start apologizing to her.

"I am so sorry, Violet. I thought that if I offered myself up, they would let you go. I never thought they would take you too."

"It's okay, Jo. As soon as that idiot put the gun to my head, I knew I would either die out in that field or they were going to take me. You should have stayed away though," she whispers as the back doors to the van are slammed shut, coating us in darkness.

"No, I would never let someone else die for me," I say sadly. Violet doesn't ask what I mean but she does make a sound of agreement. We hear the men shut the front doors of the van and then we take off.

I'm not sure how long we rode in the van for, but it must have been a while considering I fell asleep. I am jarred awake by the back doors of the van being opened.

"Out of the van," I hear Jude say. He climbs in the back and ties each of our wrists together with zip ties. He grabs Violet first, shoves her out the back door and then turns to me with a sinister smile on his face.

"The boss is going to be a very happy man tonight," he sneers as he grabs my arm in a punishing grip, sure to leave a bruise. He hauls me to my feet and pulls me out the back, right into Ryan's, Trent's second in command, arms.

I look around and realize we are at a warehouse of some sort that is surrounded by nothing but woods for miles. The outside of the building is made of metal, and I can see one door in the front with a big padlock on it. Ryan begins walking up to the door, produces a set of keys and opens it with a loud creak. I look around the inside of the building but all I can see is gray. Gray metal that makes up the walls, gray concrete floors, hell even a gray ceiling with one light hanging from it in the middle of the room.

I make eye contact with Violet, and she gives me a tiny shake of her head, indicating that she doesn't see a way out either.

Ryan and Jude walk us to the far wall, and I wince internally when I see the chains hanging from the ceiling. Jude must have seen my facial expression because he starts laughing and asks, "Brings back the memories, doesn't it Jo?"

Ryan wraps the cuffs around my wrists and locks them into place as Jude does the same to Violet. Our hands are lifted above our heads with just enough pressure on our wrists that will hurt if we try to move too much.

Suddenly, the guys step back from us as the door to the warehouse is opened and the man of my nightmares walks through whistling, looking as happy as can be.

"Well, well, I finally got my property right where it belongs," Trent laughs.

"Fuck you. I will never belong to you," I grit through my clenched jaw. Trent's face turns to stone as he balls his fists at his sides, raises one and strikes me across the cheek. I feel my skin split open where his awful gold ring connected with my face. I hold in my whimper of pain because I have handled much worse than a punch to the face.

"Stupid bitch. I bought you which makes you, my property. You belong to me, and you will do what I say when I say it," Trent snarls in my face.

"You can beat me as many times as you want. I. Don't. Belong. To. You," I enunciate every word. Trent laughs along with Ryan and Jude.

"Ah, I figured you would put up a fight. That's why I had Ryan grab your pretty little friend here too," Trent says as he walks over to Violet, stroking her cheek with the back of his hand.

"See, anytime you feel the urge to deny or disobey me, Ryan and Jude will deliver a punishment to your little friend."

Trent just ensured that I would do anything he asked me to do. I refuse to let anyone get hurt because of me.

"Now, you will receive your punishment for escaping and making me deal with even more bikers to find you," Trent nods at Ryan as he walks out of the warehouse. As soon as the door shuts, Ryan is on me, his fists hitting me what feels like everywhere.

After about 10 punches, Ryan steps back and goes after Violet. Except instead of hitting her, he starts to cut off her clothes. I can see Jude behind Ryan stripping off his own pants.

"NO," I scream. "You can't do this. I'm the one who deserves the punishment. Not her."

They both ignore me as I thrash around, trying to get their attention off Violet. My efforts are wasted when Violet screams a blood curdling scream as Jude forces himself inside of her. I try to make eye contact with her, but her expression is completely blank. It's like she is looking through me and is somewhere other than here. I close my eyes as I hear the sounds of Jude finishing and Ryan's pants unzipping. A few seconds later, I hear Violet scream again as Ryan takes his turn with her. I try to block out the noises, but it doesn't work.

After Ryan finishes, I keep my eyes closed but hear the door open and close as they leave the warehouse. I finally look over at Violet and she looks like she has no emotions. They left her naked, and she had blood running down her legs. I close my eyes as the events of the day and the beating that I took start to catch up with me.

This is all my fault.

Chapter Thirteen

Fire Burns Brighter in the Dark

Demon

I sigh as I climb off my motorcycle and walk towards my brothers. It's been three days since Jo was taken and I think I have only slept for a few hours. The first day after the girls were taken, we spent hours coming up with a plan to find their locations. We had decided to raid the Sinner's clubhouse and get the information from their President since he seems to be so close with Trent and his business.

The second day after the girls were taken was used to get surveillance on the Sinners. We needed to find the right time to take over their clubhouse. We watched their schedules and habits and found out that nightfall was our best opportunity since they loved to party all night and never really paid attention to anything else. That brings us back to now as I was up to Brute, Axle, Trigger, Brick, Viper and Ghost.

"Alright, guys. Brick, you wait for the signal and then cut all the lights. Brute and Trigger, you guys are with me going in the front. Viper and Ghost, you two are going in the back. Ghost, you are in charge of looking around for anything or anyone to do with Trent. Axle, you stick with Ghost the entire time. Once we round up Bruce and Artie, we get them to the bar area and start our questioning. Got it?' I bark my orders quickly.

They all nod once as we put in our earpieces. Brick designed all the tech shit we use, and these earpieces are small and have a microphone so we can all communicate with each other.

"Test, 1, 2, 3," Brick says into my ear. We all hold up our thumbs signaling that we can hear him.

"Alright, Brick, you stay here out of sight but keep a watch on the cameras. Let us know if anyone shows up," I say. I check to make sure I have my guns and lucky lighter and then start making my way to the tree line. We all move in tandem as we navigate our way through the mile of woods that will lead to the Sinner's clubhouse.

As we get closer, we can hear the bass of their music thumping and it confirms that they are busy partying. I stop at the edge of the tree line and look at the front door of the clubhouse.

"I see one guy manning the front door," I say into the darkness.

"We got one on the back door," Axle says.

"Alright, Brick, go ahead and cut it," I commanded.

The power shuts off and we are coated in complete silence and darkness, but we came prepared for that. I slip on my night vision glasses and make my way to the guard at the front door. I pull my gun from my waistband and fire one shot at him, taking him to the ground. I don't concern myself with seeing where I hit him. I just want to get the information on Jo, so I walk right into the clubhouse.

It's a madhouse here. I can see and hear everyone running around, trying to figure out what is happening. Little do they know; they are all meeting their makers tonight. I walk through the clubhouse, shooting every guy that I encounter. They don't even have time to react by the time that myself, Trigger or Brute fire a shot at them.

"In the front," I say as I make my way into the bar area of the clubhouse. I see naked women running for their lives and it reminds me exactly what kind of people these guys are. I may kill when warranted but I would never hurt a woman like they do. I keep an eye peeled for Bruce or Artie as I make my way towards the wall that houses the booths in the bar area.

I see Ghost making his way in and out of the rooms down the hallway to my left with Axle standing guard outside each one as he searches each of them. I give Ghost a little head nod to keep going and turn back towards the bar room. I notice a fat fucker trying to run out of the back door and I instantly recognize Bruce from the pictures that Jo showed me. I make my way to him, looping my arm around his neck and squeezing so he can't escape my hold. He lets out the loudest girlish scream I have ever heard come out of a man's mouth.

"I have Bruce by the back door," I announced to my brothers.

"We've got Artie by the bedrooms," Trigger says.

"Good, turn the lights back on Brick. Bring Artie to the bar to see his father," I say as I start dragging Bruce to a chair in the middle of the room. I sit him down and tie his hands to each arm rest and his legs to the legs of the chair. As the lights turn back on, I remove my glasses and look at the fat fuck that my Jo was tormented by. He is a chubby little guy with a greasy, bald head and an extremely red face. Oh, little man is pissed.

A few seconds later, Trigger and Brute come into the bar area with a naked Artie struggling against them, his dick just flopping around. I let out a little laugh as they sat him in the chair next to Bruce and tied him down.

"We found him in his room with a girl tied to the bed. She was crying and screaming that she didn't want to do this," Trigger growls.

My face instantly turns murderous when I hear about Artie's activities. It reminds me of why we are here, and that Jo was taken from me because of these two nasty fuckers.

"What the fuck do you want?" Bruce finally speaks. He tries to sound mad, but I can see the fear in his eyes when he looks at me. He must have heard of my reputation. I didn't get the President patch and name Demon for nothing.

"What do we want? We are looking for your little buddy Trent. You know, the one who buys and sells girls," I spit at him.

Bruce throws his head back and laughs, increasing my need to put a bullet in his head.

"What do you need with Trent? You need to buy a woman? We've got plenty here. There was no need to tie us up with all the dramatics," Bruce laughs.

"No, fucker, unlike you, we don't have to force a woman to pretend to want us. Trent took my girl and I want her back. Since you are obviously so close with him, you can tell me where he took her," I say through gritted teeth. I am about one comment away from ending this fat fucker's life.

"What girl?" Bruce questions.

"That's none of your fucking business," Trigger says from behind me. I know he's looking out for Jo's safety since we agreed to try and keep Jo's name away from this bullshit.

"I don't know where Trent is, so you wasted your time," Bruce says.

I look over at Artie and his eyes widen when I smile my devilish smile at him. We already anticipated Bruce not giving up Trent. It is the reason why we took Artie too. I reach into my pocket for my favorite lighter and pull it out. Trigger hands me a bottle of vodka from the bar. I turn to Artie and ask, "Now, we figured Pops here wouldn't give up Trent's location so would you like to tell us or find out why they call me Demon?"

Artie's eyes widen even more as he shakes his head and says, "I have no idea. Only dad always knows his location."

"Bummer. This is probably going to hurt a lot," I say as I pour the vodka all over Artie's little dick that is just lying there.

"Dad! You're just going to let them light my dick on fire for Trent?" Artie screams while thrashing, trying to get away from the lighter I am currently playing with. Taunting him seems to be working for the moment. Hopefully, he can get his dad to tell us where Trent is keeping Jo and Violet.

Bruce looks away from his son and says quietly, "He will kill me if I tell them anything."

"Who gives a fuck? They are going to light me on fucking fire," Artie yells.

Bruce shakes his head, so I walk over to him, grabbing him by the hair, wrenching his head back. I get close to his face and say, "You are a fucking piece of shit. Willing to let your son be lit on fire for some guy who would kill you without blinking."

"He would not," Bruce argues.

Every single one of my men, including myself, laughed loudly at his exclamation.

"Oh, but he would. Want to know how I know that? I watched Trent take out his own brother with a bullet to the head just for contradicting him one time. You think you are special to him?" Trigger says. I look back at him and he just shrugs his shoulders. I will have to come back to that with him later.

"Enough," I bellow. "Now, either tell us where Trent is, or Artie here will lose his tiny little dick and meet the Devil a lot sooner than he planned."

"I got them Pres. Bruce had his phone in his office with Trent's location on it. They are at a warehouse about 20 miles from here," Ghost says in my ear. I smile because I finally know where my Princess is, and I am going to rescue her.

"Alright boys, you heard Ghost. We have their locations. Let's light it up," I yell at all my men. Trigger, Brute, and Viper start grabbing bottles of alcohol and pouring them all over the room. I grab the bottle of vodka I had earlier and pour it all over Artie and Bruce. They are going down with this place.

"Wait, if you have your girl's location, why are you still lighting us on fire?" Artie screams.

"This is for Jo and all of the bullshit you put her through growing up in this sorry excuse for a motorcycle club," I say as I punch Bruce in the face. He spits his blood on the floor and then looks back at me and laughs loudly.

"Jo? That whore is who you are doing all of this for?"

I clench my fists and am about to start beating the shit out of this fat fuck when Grizzly comes out of nowhere and stands behind Bruce with a knife pressed to his neck. Bruce instantly stops laughing and all of the blood drains from his face.

"This is for Brianna. You killed her because she was trying to leave your pathetic ass. And this is for Jo, my daughter, that you tortured for years," Grizzly says as he drags the knife across Bruce's neck. The cut is so deep that blood sprays everywhere and his head almost comes clean off his shoulders. Grizzly stands there panting until Artie makes a whimper sound, drawing Grizzly's attention to him. Grizzly turns and says, "Your turn. Jo was your little plaything so now it is time for you to be mine."

Grizzly walks to Artie and picks up his limp dick, places his knife on it and starts sawing it off. I wince because that makes my own dick shrivel up. I thought I was named Demon but with what Grizzly just did, maybe I should think about giving him that road name. Artie screams and then passes out. Grizzly throws his severed dick across the room and then turns to me.

"Sorry Pres. I couldn't just sit at the clubhouse knowing these fuckers were here after everything they did to Brianna and Jo," Grizzly apologizes.

"It's all good, Grizz. Just don't touch me with that hand until you scrub it. I don't know what kind of diseases that nasty fucker had," I reply.

Grizzly throws his head back and laughs. I shake my head at him and then turn around to my men. They are all looking at Grizzly with a new respect. Family means everything in this world and Grizzly sticking up for his family has gained him the respect of every man in this room.

"Alright, let's light this place up guys. I'm ready to go get my girl," I yell.

We all make our way to the front door of the clubhouse, stepping over all the dead members of the Sinners. I use a bottle of alcohol to pour a line to the front door and then step outside. I turn back around, lighting my lucky lighter, and tossing it into the puddle. I watch as the fire catches and then turn to make my way back the mile long walk to our bikes. Time for me to go rescue my Princess.

Chapter Fourteen

Love Rescued Me

Jo

It has been days of torture in this metal prison box. Every day, we start the day with either a beating or I have to listen to Violet get violated. She stopped talking completely after the second time they forced her. I think she has put her mind in a different place. The guys never touch me sexually, but they love to put bruises and cuts on my skin.

The door to the warehouse opens and I squint against the harsh moonlight that pours in. Trent walks into the metal prison. I have not seen him since the first day we got here but I knew he would be back at some point. He looks pissed in his crumpled suit. His dark hair looks unwashed and like he has been constantly running his fingers through it.

"You. You are too much trouble and not worth it," Trent snarls as he points at me. He must register the bruises and cuts from his henchmen because as his eyes scan up and down my body, he relaxes and smiles.

"Ryan and Jude really did a number on you," he laughs.

Speak of the Devil and he shall appear. The door opens again and in walks Ryan and Jude. I glance at Violet, and she is just staring at the wall in front of her, a vacant look on her face.

"Your little biker boyfriend decided to cross the wrong guy. I think it's time to teach him a lesson," Trent says.

Derrick. Demon. Gosh, I miss him. I have thought about him the entire time I have been in this prison. I hoped he would find me but after a couple of days, I gave up hoping that he would be able to find us. I knew Trent was smart so he would have hidden our locations.

Trent pulls a knife out of his suit pocket and walks over to me. He grabs my shirt and starts cutting it off me, but he cuts into my skin too. I let out a scream, but he ignores me. Next, he cuts my pants in two long slices down each side of my legs. I feel a burning pain as my skin separates at the same time my clothes do. I start crying as Trent moves to make deep slices on my forearm. After he is done, I look up and see that he carved his name into my arm, and it is bleeding heavily.

Trent steps back to admire his handy work and smiles once he sees what he's accomplished. He walks back over to the chain holding me up and lets me drop to the floor. I hit the concrete hard and the breath is knocked out of my body. Trent kicks my ribs and tells me to get to my knees. I must take too long because I see Jude walk over to Violet. I immediately push myself onto my knees because I cannot let Violet go through another raping. As soon as I get on my knees, Trent wrenches my head back by my hair and then proceeds to unbutton and unzip his pants. I close my eyes to avoid looking at him when he does what I know he plans to do.

"I am going to get some use out of you before I kill you and send your body back to your beloved biker," Trent snarls in my ear. He pulls my hair harder, causing tears to gather behind my eyelids and I feel one drop down my cheek.

"Now, open wide," Trent commands.

I am so sorry Derrick; I think as I open my mouth. I feel Trent force himself inside of my mouth, shoving so hard that I gag. Trent starts laughing as I try to not throw up at the smell of his body odor emanating from his crotch. I feel myself start sobbing as Trent pulls out and finishes in my hair. I lay down on the ground and just let out gut wrenching sobs.

Suddenly, the warehouse door is ripped open, but I do not bother to open my eyes and see who came in. I lay on the ground, eyes closed, crying when I felt arms wrap around me and Derrick's voice in my ear.

"Shh, it's okay baby. I'm here now Princess. I've got you," he whispers as he holds me tightly to his body. I start to sob harder at the relief I feel to finally be in his arms again. I cry for the fact that I just lost a part of myself to what Trent just forced me to do. I cry for the beatings I endured again. I just keep crying.

"Oh, God, Violet. What have they done to you baby?" I hear Viper whisper and I finally open my eyes. I look around and see all of the high-ranking members of the Blue Devils standing around the warehouse, looking around in disgust. I see Brute and Trigger tying up Ryan and Jude, Axle is helping Viper get Violet's chains off, Ghost is standing in the corner silently, and Grizzly is standing next to me on guard. I don't see Trent anywhere, but I assume the guys already got him.

I turn to look at Derrick and I can see the worry on his face. I have no idea what he is thinking right now but I am just so relieved to be in his arms again.

"Pres, we need to get them to the hospital," Viper says.

I forgot I was hurt for a few seconds because I was so distracted by the fact that Derrick came for me. But now that Viper said something, I feel the pain radiating down my arm. I had it covered when Derrick started holding me, so he hasn't seen it yet. He must have noticed where my eyes went because he flips my arm over and sees Trent's name carved into my arm.

"Oh, baby, no. I am so sorry," He whispers as he kisses my forehead. I start to feel dizzy as the past few days hit me and my adrenaline begins to wear off. I look at Derrick once more and say, "I knew you would come for me. I had hoped you would."

Right before I pass out, I hear him say, "You are mine, Princess. I will always come for you."

Chapter Fifteen

Bad News Travels Fast

Demon

When Jo passes out in my arms, I jump into action. I stand up with her and rush out of the door of the warehouse they were being kept at.

"We need to get them to the hospital now," I commanded. Thankfully, Grizzly was smart enough to bring a van because there is no way the girls could ride on a bike in their conditions. I slide into the back seat of the van with Jo in my lap. Viper slides in next to me with Violet in his lap, closes the door and then tells Grizzly to go.

I look down at Jo and notice all her injuries. She is bleeding on her arm where that bastard carved his name into her, and she has some cuts down her sides. I can only imagine the hell they went through.

"Violet, baby, can you hear me? I am so sorry," I hear Viper whisper. I saw the injuries Violet had and the look on her face. She went through something horrible, and I hope for her and Viper's sake that she can recover from it. He is as gone for her as I am for Jo.

My phone starts ringing but I ignore it. I focus completely on Jo and making sure she keeps breathing. Grizzly's phone starts ringing next, and he answers it. He listens to the person on the other end and then turns his attention to me. I can tell by the look on his face that I am not going to like what comes out of his mouth.

"Pres, Trent escaped. They have the other two that were in the warehouse and need to know what you want to do with them," he says regretfully.

"Fuck, okay. Tell them to take them to the basement and we will deal with them when we can," I tell him.

Grizzly relays the message and then hangs up the phone as we pull into the hospital parking lot. Viper gets out with Violet, and I follow suit holding Jo tightly to my chest. I walk up to a nurse and explain that my girl needs to be seen now. She takes one look at Jo and orders a gurney for her. Once I place her on the gurney, the hospital staff starts to wheel her to the back. I try to follow but I am stopped by a nurse putting her hand on my chest. I step back out of her reach because no woman except mine gets to touch me.

"Sorry sir, you need to wait out here while we assess your friend," she says, putting emphasis on the word friend.

"That's my wife in there. I will be joining her," I spit out.

"Then I will call security. I don't see a ring on your finger, nor did I see one on her finger. So, I don't believe you are married. Go sit in the waiting room," she says.

Viper walks up behind me and barks at the snarky bitch, "Watch your mouth talking about our President's Old Lady."

The nurse opens her mouth to say something but before she can speak, I cut her off.

"Where is your supervisor? I don't want you anywhere near my wife or her care."

Suddenly, the double doors behind the snarky nurse open and an older man in a white lab coat comes out, heading straight for us. I guess we are making a scene.

"What is going on here?" he questions, raising his eyebrows when he notices our Blue Devils cuts.

I point to the nurse and say, "I don't want her anywhere near my wife. She thought hitting on me while refusing to let me sit with my wife was going to earn her a ride with a biker."

Viper lets out a small laugh and I see the doctor's lips turn up at the corners. Snarky's face turns red with embarrassment as she tries to defend herself.

"I was telling him that he had to wait in the waiting room while we looked at his friend," she says.

"See, I have told you twice that she is my wife, but you continue to call her my friend. I may not wear a ring, but that woman back there is mine and it would be in your best interest to remember that," I growl.

"Okay, Natalie, that's enough. Go home for the night," the doctor tells Snarky. She huffs and stomps off.

"I know how Old Ladies work in your world but at this hospital, if you are not legally married then I can't let you back there right now. You can wait in the waiting room, and I will personally see to your woman's care and update you myself," the doctor says.

"Thanks doctor," I shake his hand and lead Viper back to the waiting room. I sit in the uncomfortable plastic chair and rest my head in my hands.

"I don't know how Violet will come back from this Pres. She had no emotions and refused to talk to anyone, even the hospital workers," Viper says.

"I don't know Viper, but you need to be there for her. She's going to need you," I tell him. He nods his head and sits in the chair next to mine.

We wait for hours, and all our brothers show up for our women. The waiting room is filled with the entire Blue Devils Motorcycle Club when the older doctor comes through the double doors. I jump to my feet, and he meets me in the middle of the room.

"I came to update you on Ms. Week's condition, but I think we should talk privately. I also put myself on Ms. Phillips' case so if her Old Man would like to join us, then follow me," he says as Viper and I follow him through a doorway to our left. We come into a small sitting room with a couch, television and coffee maker.

"Why all the secrecy, doctor?" I ask impatiently.

"I didn't think all of your men should hear about what injuries I found on both girls," he says quietly. I grab the arm of the couch in a punishing grip to prepare myself.

"I will start with Ms. Weeks. She had a lot of bruising and cuts on her body. Several required stitches so we stitched them up and gave her something for the pain. Before she fell asleep, I asked her if she would be okay with me sharing what else we found with you, and she gave her permission. We found semen in her hair and tearing in her mouth and throat," the doctor says, apologetically.

"You are telling me one of those bastards forced my girl to suck his dick?" I yell. The doctor winces at my raised voice but gives me a small nod. I take deep breaths, trying to stop myself from leaving right now to put a bullet in their heads.

"I am very sorry. Now for Ms. Phillips. Her injuries were much more severe. She had violent tearing and bruising in her vaginal walls. We performed a pregnancy test as part of the rape kit, and it came back positive, so we did an ultrasound. It was determined that the fetus had died approximately three days ago so we performed an emergency dilation and curettage to remove the fetus," the doctor starts explaining the medical language. I look over at Viper and see pure devastation on his face.

"She was pregnant? She was violently raped, and the baby died?" Viper asks.

"I am so sorry son, yes."

"FUCK!" Viper yells and throws the coffee maker across the room. It hits the wall and explodes everywhere. He goes for the television next, but I race over to him and grab him, pinning his arms behind his back until he drops to the ground. He throws his head back and lets out a loud yell and then starts sobbing into his hands. I see movement and notice the doctor slowly making his way out of the room but stops before he completely exits.

"When you are ready, let the nurse know to take you to the back."

I nod my head at him as I watch Viper completely lose his shit and start panting. Most men think it makes you a pussy to cry but after what Viper just learned, I do not blame him at all. After a few minutes, Viper jumps up from the floor and says, "I gotta go, Pres."

"Are you coming back?" I ask him.

"Yeah, yeah. I just need a minute," he says.

Viper walks out of the room, and I follow behind him. He does not stop as he rushes out of the emergency room door, and I do not stop to talk to anyone either. I make my way to the nurse's desk and tell her I want to see my wife. She directs me to room 12 and I stop outside her door to take a deep breath and prepare myself to see my Princess.

Chapter Sixteen

Sometimes Home is a Person

Jo

Beep. Beep. Beep.

I wake up to the most annoying beeping noise that I have ever heard. I groan as I try to move my arm to shut it up and a sharp pain radiates down my forearm. I risk opening my eyes and immediately regret it when bright lights assault my vision.

"Princess?" I hear a voice ask. Wait, I know that voice. Derrick. I risk opening my eyes again, slowly this time and see Derrick sitting on the edge of the leather chair in my hospital room. It takes me a few minutes to realize why I am here and then the memories come flooding back. I let out a whimper as I tried not to think about what Trent made me do to him.

The bed shifts and I feel Derrick's arms enclose me in. I relax as he strokes my hair and whispers in my ear.

"You are safe baby. They can't hurt you anymore. I am right here with you."

I calm down after a few minutes and turn to look at Derrick. He has dark circles under his eyes and his clothes are crumpled.

"How long have I been out? How long have you been here?" I ask him.

"Two days," he answers as he kisses the top of my head. I lean in and press my lips to his, needing him to replace the repulsive memories. Our lips slide together as he deepens the kiss. I let out a little moan at the contact and Derrick immediately pulled back.

"Baby, you just went through some traumatic shit," he says.

"I am sorry," I say, looking away from his face. I can't survive seeing the disappointment on his face.

He grabs my chin between his fingers and forces my eyes back to his.

"Princess, never apologize for kissing me. You can kiss me anytime you want. I just want to make sure you are okay," he says, placing a gentle peck to my lips.

"I am okay, Derrick. I just had some flashbacks."

"Whenever you are ready, you can talk to me about it, baby," he tells me gently.

I nod my head at him as the door to my hospital room opens and in walks my doctor.

"Hello, Ms. Weeks. How are you feeling today?" Doctor Massengill asks.

"I am okay. I have a little bit of pain but that is it," I tell him, hoping to get out of this place because I hate hospitals.

"That is to be expected. I am going to look at your wounds and if everything looks good, you can go home today," Doctor Massengill tells me as he peels back the bandage on my forearm. I swing my eyes to the ceiling, so I do not have to see Trent's name scarred into my skin.

"Oh, I forgot to mention, when we were stitching up your arm, one of my nurses had a mishap with the scalpel. She accidentally cut your skin and had to sew it back in a different way," the doctor states. I look at him in confusion until I notice the long zig-zag pattern of stitches that cover my forearm, running right over Trent's name. My eyes fill with tears as I look at the doctor and thank him quietly. He winks at me and then proceeds to check the rest of my cuts along my sides and legs. He declares that I am fit to be released today but on strict orders to take it easy, so I do not risk busting any of the stitches open.

"That will not be a problem, doctor," Derrick tells him and winks at me. I roll my eyes because I already know that he is going to force me to lay in bed the entire time I am healing.

The doctor leaves the room so I can change into clothes that somehow appeared in my room.

"Grizzly brought us some clean clothes to wear back to the clubhouse. I figured you didn't want to go home in a hospital gown," Derrick says.

"More like you don't ant to risk any of the guys seeing me in a gown that doesn't close in the back," I laugh at him.

"Damn right. You are mine. No one gets to see you except me," he declares.

"Oh, so you just get to decide that I am yours? Don't I get a say?"

Derrick stops in his tracks to the bathroom to took at me curiously. He lifts his eyebrow and asks, "You saying you don't want to be mine?"

I immediately shake my head and say, “Of course I want to be yours. If you are mine. I don’t share.”

Derrick walks back to the bed, leans over and plants a kiss on my lips.

“Good, neither do I,” he says.

Derrick helps me stand up and change into soft flannel pants and a Blue Devil’s oversized shirt. His smell hits my nose as the shirt settles on my chest. I take a deep breath, inhaling his scent. He is helping me put on my shoes as the nurse wheels in a wheelchair. We get my shoes on and then he helps me waddle over to the wheelchair and sit down in it. The pain medication they gave me is making me a bit woozy.

“I have got it from here,” Derrick says as he grabs the handle on the back of the chair and begins to wheel me out of the room. Once we get down the hallway and out the sliding doors, I see every member of the Blue Devils Motorcycle Club standing beside their bikes. They are all parked in a formation, Axle leading, and a van in the middle surrounded. They instantly start cheering as Derrick wheels me to the passenger seat of the van.

“What is all of this?” I ask, looking around at all the guys as they start to mount their bikes.

“This is them showing their support for their President’s Old Lady,” Derrick says as he puts his arms under my legs and back and lifts me into the passenger seat. He leans over and clicks my seat belt into place. I grab his face and place a big kiss on his lips.

“What was that for?” he asks.

“That was for everything you have done for me. You rescued me and now I feel like I finally have the family that I have always wanted,” I tell him earnestly.

"You will always have me and the club at your backs Jo. You are a part of this as much as I am," he says.

I smile at him and watch as he closes my door, rounds the front of the van and slides into the driver's seat. I turn to look at him and notice how handsome he is even with his two-day stubble and tired eyes. Derrick catches me staring and gives me a wink as everyone starts up their engines. Derrick rolls down his window and sticks his thumb up, signaling that we are ready to go. I look around once more.

Home. This, these people, this place, is my home.

Chapter Seventeen

The Truth Hurts

Jo

We arrived back at the clubhouse and Derrick let me say hello as he carried me bridal style to our room and deposited me in bed. After feeding me and changing my bandages, we started watching television together when there was a loud knock at the door. Derrick got up to open the door but before he could reach it, the door swung open to reveal a panting Grizzly.

"What the fuck?" Derrick yells.

"Sorry, Pres. I heard Jo woke up and came back today and I wanted to see her for myself. Make sure she was okay," Grizzly says, walking into the room.

"I am fine, Dad. I promise. Demon here will not let me lift one finger," I roll my eyes at him.

"Dad? That's the first time you have called me that," Grizzly's voice has turned hoarse.

"Yeah, well you are my dad and it just slipped out," I say sheepishly, embarrassed that he is making a big deal out of it.

"Okay, I won't say anything else about it other than it means so much to me that you think of me that way," Grizzly says as he sits in the leather recliner next to the bed. Derrick just stares at him with narrowed eyes.

"Grizzly. You have seen Jo. She is fine. You can go now," Derrick says. Grizzly looks away from the movie playing on the television for a brief second before returning his attention to the movie.

"No thanks. I think I want to spend some time with my daughter. You can stay if you want to," Grizzly says.

Derrick growls at him but stomps out of the room and announces that he is going to get me some dessert. I laugh at him because he doesn't need to be jealous of my father. We watch the movie for a little while before Grizzly mutes the television and turns his attention to me.

"How are you really doing, sweetheart? You can always be honest with me. I won't judge you if you are not okay," he says.

I think about it for a minute. Am I okay?

"That is a tough question to answer right now. Am I okay? Physically, yes. Mentally and emotionally is an entirely different story but I don't want to bother Derrick, I mean Demon, with my emotional problems. He already has enough shit on his plate," I reply, swinging my gaze to the ceiling.

"Talk to me about it. I can be an unbiased opinion," he jokes.

I take a deep breath and then start talking to my dad about my problems.

"I don't know what they all told you I went through while I was held captive. I didn't have it as bad as Violet did but I still went through some crazy shit. I was chained up for days, taking beatings every single day. I could handle all that better than I thought. I thought I would make it out unscathed, well as unscathed as I could be. Then Trent showed up around an hour before you guys did, and he forced me to do things to him. I don't know how I can come back from that. I keep having nightmares about it," I whisper.

I notice Grizzly gripping the arm rests of the chair so hard his knuckles are white. He takes a deep breath and then tells me something that will forever change my life.

"I know you didn't know your mother very well when she died but I did. Do you know why she was with that fucker Bruce?" Grizzly asks. I shake my head no because I could never understand why she stayed with that man.

"It's because he had bought her. When I first met your mother, she was at the grocery store buying food for the Sinners clubhouse. She accidentally bumped into me with her shopping cart, which is funny considering I am a huge guy and she tried to say she didn't see me," he laughs. Seeing the smile on his face when he talks about my mother makes me realize how much he loved her.

"Anyways, I met her, and we started talking. I couldn't get her to trust me for the longest time, but I was very persistent. I came back to that grocery store almost every single day until I saw her again. Finally, she told me that she was being held against her will at that clubhouse. I made it my mission to help her escape. My President at the time was willing to help so we had come up with a plan to help her get out of there. We were set to get her out the next day, but she came to me that night and told me goodbye. She said she couldn't leave him anymore because she had fallen in love with Bruce. I knew it was bullshit but if she didn't want to leave, there was nothing I could do. We made you that night as we said goodbye. I never saw her again after that. But I think she was raped by Bruce later that night and didn't really know who your father was, so she stayed with the guy who, even though he hurt her, provided for you," Grizzly is tearing up by the end of the story. I grab his hand and hold it. I don't say anything else and neither does he. We just sit there and comfort each other as we experience the loss of the woman and mother that we loved.

After a few hours of bonding time, Derrick returns to the room and Grizzly makes his exit, saying he will visit with me as much as possible. I lay down and try to draw from my mother's strength to get through these nightmares. I eventually drift off to sleep and it is the first night I sleep all the way through the night without dreaming of that horrific event.

Chapter Eighteen

True Friendship is Never Serene

Jo

It has been two weeks since I came home from the hospital and today is the day that Violet is coming home so I am currently getting myself dressed. I am standing in the bathroom drying my hair when I hear a knock on the door. I open it to see Grizzly standing there with his hands tucked into his front pocket.

"Pres told me to come escort you to Violet's room," he says.

I roll my eyes because this has been a constant thing, Derrick sending someone else to talk to me or escort me somewhere. I have barely seen him much less talked to him myself. I can't help but think that he is avoiding me because of what I told him happened with Trent. We sat in bed on the second night that I was home, and I told him everything. Ever since, he has avoided me. Maybe he just doesn't want me anymore.

"Give me like five minutes and I will be ready to go," I tell Grizzly.

"Sure thing. I will be sitting in the chair out here waiting," he says as he walks over to the recliner in the corner of the room. I close the bathroom door and finishing drying my hair and then putting it up into a ponytail. I walk back out into the room and Grizzly stands up to walk with me. I am walking better than I was, without assistance but it still hurts to walk a long distance. We walk out of the door and Grizzly turns right down the hallway, leading towards Viper's room. We stop outside of the door and Grizzly knocks on the door.

"Come in," I hear Viper yell as we open the door to enter. I see Viper first, sitting in a recliner like Derrick's next to the bed. Violet is sitting on the bed staring at the wall with a blank look on her face. Viper gets up from his seat and offers it to me.

"Okay, I will leave you two ladies alone to bond or whatever the fuck chicks do," he says as he and Grizzly walk back out of the door. I look over Violet and she looks super thin, like she hasn't eaten the entire time she has been in the hospital. As far as I know, she developed an infection from the baby and had to stay for a course of antibiotics which is why it took her so long to come home.

"Hey Violet. It's Jo. I don't know why I just announced myself like you can't see me," I say, my hands trembling. I take a deep breath and let everything I wanted to say come out, in one big mess of words.

"I am so sorry for what you went through. I feel like this is all my fault. I brought Trent and his goons here and none of what you went through would have happened if I had just kept running that night instead of accepting that ride from you. I know what you went through was hard, wait, that's not the right word, it was a clusterfuck of bullshit, and I am so sorry that you went through any of that. I just want you to know that I am here for you. I know you haven't talked to anyone about what happened. Or talked at all but just know that I am here if you need someone to talk to," I ramble on.

Violet holds up her hand to stop me. "Jo," she says hoarsely. She looks at me with tears in her eyes and rolling down her cheeks. I grab her hand and hold it tight in mine.

"This is not your fault. You didn't do anything to me. Those bastards did. They were the ones to force me to have sex with them when I didn't want to. They are the ones who killed my child. Not you. I do not blame you for any of this. I haven't spoken to anyone because I can hardly look at Viper without being reminded of the child that we lost. I also have a constant loop of every time those guys touched me running in my head, so it is either I am silent, or I cry every single day, all day. Please don't take this the wrong way but I don't need anyone to talk to right now. I am trying to sort out so much shit in my head and I need to do it alone," she says, tears running steadily down her cheeks.

"Okay. I support you no matter what you need. If you want to be left alone, that is okay. I can respect that. Just know I am here for whenever you do need me, okay? You are like my best friend, scratch that, you are my best friend, and I will be here through anything and everything with you," I tell her.

"Thank you. I will let you know if I need anything," she says as she wipes her face and goes back to staring at the wall with no emotions on her face again. I get up and walk to the door, stopping one last time to look at Violet. She gives me a small nod of the head and I walk out of the door and straight into Viper's back.

"Oomph," I say as I fall backwards onto the floor. I let out a little yelp as my cut leg hits the floor.

"Oh fuck, I am so sorry Jo. I didn't know you were going to high tail it out of there like that," Viper exclaims as he helps me off the floor.

"It's fine Viper. Violet said she wanted to be alone, so I left," I tell him. He looks at me in shock for a second before shaking his head.

"She talked to you. Like said actual words?" he questions.

"Yes. She did but I can't tell you what she said. Just take it easy on her, okay? She has been through a lot," I tell him as I walk towards Grizzly. He lifts me into his arms and carries me back to Derrick's bedroom.

"Thank you. Falling did not do my healing any good," I tell him as he puts me on the bed.

"Anything for you, daughter. You okay after your talk with Violet?" he asks me gently.

"Yeah, I am okay. I just feel so bad for Violet. I know she is strong, but I don't know if she will get through this alone," I voice my worries to my dad.

"Some people just deal with trauma differently baby girl. You cling to people when you go through something, and others like Violet, push people away. We just need to keep a check on her and make sure she doesn't get too far into her own head," he says.

"You are right dad. Thanks for talking to me about this."

"Anytime. Now let's get you fed and some rest. You still need to heal a little more," he says as he pulls his phone out to order the prospect to get us some food. We talk and watch television for a few hours before I fall asleep in the middle of a movie, wondering what is going to happen with Violet and Derrick. My life is all types of complicated.

Chapter Nineteen

An Eye for An Eye

Demon

I am sitting in my office at the clubhouse, thinking of Jo when Grizzly bursts through the door without knocking. I raise my eyebrows at him because he knows better than to just rush in here without announcing himself. He is lucky I don't have my gun in reach, or he would be wearing a little hole in his chest.

"Sorry, Pres. I forgot to knock," he says as he rubs the back of his neck.

"It's fined this time. Just remember to knock next time or I am not going to be responsible for my actions if I accidentally shoot you," I tell him. He throws his head back and laughs like I was making a joke. I was not.

"Gotcha, anyways, I just left Jo asleep in your room. She went and talked to Violet today," he says.

I cringe at the fact that I had to send Grizzly to take her to see Violet. I was supposed to be the one to do it but I had to get a deal made with another club on a shipment of guns and didn't have the time to make it up there. Hopefully, she understands that I am the President of a motorcycle club which can be a busy job.

"How did that go?" I ask him.

"Well as far as I know, Violet spoke to Jo but other than that, I have no idea what she said. Jo will not tell anyone what she said. She said something about girl code or some shit," he rolls his eyes and huffs as he sits in the chair across from my desk. I nod my head at him just as my door swings open again and Viper walks into my office like he owns the place.

"Doesn't anyone know the concept of fucking knocking anymore?" I growl at Viper.

"Nope. I just came to say that I am going to the basement to take care of the bastards that hurt my woman and killed my child," he announces and then walks back out of my office. I look at Grizzly and we both jump out of our seats at the same time to follow Viper.

"Viper," I yell as he reaches the door to the basement, located behind the bar.

He stops walking and leans his head against the door. He takes a deep breath and then says, "I can't keep living like this Pres. They are sitting down here in this basement and now that Violet is back, I refuse to have them living under the same roof as her."

"I wasn't going to stop you. I just wanted to join. I want a few of my own hits since they were the ones who beat my Old Lady," I say.

Grizzly turns to me with a smile on his face. "Old Lady huh?" he asks.

I nod at him and then turn my focus back to Viper. He shrugs his shoulders and throws open the basement door. I follow him down the long staircase that opens into a soundproof concrete room with a drain in the middle of the floor. I look over both guys who look like they are enjoying their stay in this basement a little too much. I notice Grizzly standing off to the side, leaning up against the wall with his arms crossed over his chest and glaring at the two men we have chained to the ceiling the same way the girls were. We decided in a Church meeting that it would be Viper and I to end the bastard's lives since they fucked with our women.

I watch as Viper walks to the metal cabinet on the right side of the room that houses his special blades and smile. These fuckers have no idea what they are in store for. I walk over to the other metal cabinet on the left side of the room that houses my blow torches. I pick one up and walk over to the smaller of the two men. Viper picks out his most prized blade that has a snake wrapped around the handle and walks over to the bigger of the two.

"What's your name?" Viper growls in his face. The guy just laughs and seals his lips shut. I know from the story Jo told me exactly what his name is, so I inform Viper that the one he is standing in front of is named Jude. He smiles a devilish smile at the man, and I watch as Jude's eyes widen with fear.

"So, you are the one who touched my woman the most? This is going to be so much fun for me. See, they call me Viper for a reason. You want to know the reason?" He taunts Jude as he uses his regular pocketknife to slice through Jude's shirt. Jude shakes his head no.

"I am going to tell you anyways. They call me Viper because my favorite weapon to kill someone with is a blade dipped in viper venom. The blade cuts and the viper venom eats away at the human cells, causing a very slow and painful death," Viper tells him and I watch all of the blood drain from Jude's face.

Viper just laughs as he makes his first cut into Jude's chest and Jude lets out a high-pitched scream. I watch as Viper make shallow enough cuts to not let Jude bleed out but deep enough to get the viper venom into his system. After he finishes carving the head of a snake into Jude's chest, he returns his knife to the metal cabinet and steps back to watch Jude die slowly.

I pick up my blow torch and walk over to Ryan who looks like he is about to piss his pants.

"Since you decided to put a gun to my head and kidnap my Old Lady and beat her, it's your turn," I say as I smile at Ryan's fear.

"See, Viper got his name the same way I did. We were named for our weapon choices. They call me demon because I love to play with fire," I warn him as I turn my blow torch on. I don't even bother cutting Ryan's clothes off because I am just going to burn them off. I raise my torch to his face and get close enough where he can feel the heat coming off it. He tries to jerk his head away, but he can't go very far with the chains attached to his wrists.

I finally touch the blow torch to Ryan's face, burning his eyes out of his head. He screams but passes out quickly. I add my signature of burning the letter D into his chest. I stand back with Viper and Grizzly as we watch both men die slowly. After the life has drained out of them, I call the prospect down to clean up and get rid of the bodies.

I head back up the stairs and grab a drink at the bar. Taking a life always takes something out of me, even if they deserve it.

Chapter Twenty

Trust The Timing

Demon

I think something is seriously wrong with Jo. It has been a month since she came home from the hospital and every day after the first week, she has been snapping at me. I have no idea what is wrong with her, but I plan to find out. Every time I ask her what is wrong, she tells me she is fine, but I know my woman, and something is definitely wrong.

I walk out of the kitchen and into our bar area to find Jo sitting in a booth, laughing at something Brute, my VP, has said to her. A wave of jealousy hits my body so hard that I have to clench my hands into fists. I march over to the booth and growl, "What the fuck is going on here?"

Brute and Jo look startled by my presence, only fueling my anger. Brute throws his hands up in front of him and slowly gets up from the table.

"Nothing is going on, Pres. I was just talking to Jo about some things she had questions about," he says. I narrow my eyes at him and am about to tell him to fuck off when Jo finally explodes all her anger on me.

"Demon," I wince at her calling me by my road name, "you have no right to come in here acting like some alpha male bullshit when you have barely talked to me in weeks. Brute was answering some of my questions I had about your MC world since I couldn't find you, yet again."

I stare at Jo and probably look as confused as I feel because she narrows her eyes at me and her face morphs into a very angry woman. Does she think I have just been avoiding her?

"Wait a second, that is what has been bothering you this whole time? You think I have been avoiding you on purpose?" I ask her for clarification.

She nods her head at me. I turn to see that all my guys have stopped what they were doing to watch the show. Jo must notice too because her face turns bright red with embarrassment. I will not have my woman feel like she cannot talk to me. I yell for everyone to get out. They all drop whatever they were doing and run out of the main room. I turn back to Jo and go to take a step towards her, but she takes a step back and holds up her hand, signaling for me to stop. Her pulling away from me sends a sharp pain shooting through my chest.

"Jo, baby, Princess. I was not avoiding you. I was trying to let you heal and rest and then I had a lot of club business to take care of."

She rolls her eyes and says, "Do not give me that bullshit Derrick. The doctor cleared me a week ago for normal activities."

"Yes, but you were still having nightmares and I did not want to make anything worse for you," I tell her gently.

Apparently, Jo has had enough because she is suddenly crying and yelling, waving her hands animatedly as she yells at me.

"You think me having nightmares means I wanted you to leave me alone? NO. What I needed was YOU Derrick. I needed you to hold me or touch me. I needed you to replace the bad memories with your good ones. If my scars are too much…"

I cut off that idiotic statement by slamming my mouth down on hers. She instantly responds by throwing her arms around my neck and letting out a deep moan when my tongue touches hers. We stand there devouring one another until my cock is so hard, I can barely stand it. I pull back and rest my forehead on hers.

"You never have to worry about me not wanting you, Princess," I say as I press my hard length into her side. "I will always want you. That is why I was trying to give you space to heal so I could finally make you mine."

She lets out a moan and then says the words I have been waiting to hear, "Take me to our room, Derrick. Make me yours, please."

I instantly place my hands on her ass and lift her up, encouraging her to wrap her legs around my waist. She latches her mouth onto mine and starts grinding against my length as I walk us down the hallway towards our room. I stop at our door and Jo moves to kiss down my neck so I can unlock and open the door. As soon as the door closes behind us, I slam her against the wall, pinning her hips with mine and grinding my hard cock on her. I trail kisses down her neck until I lick a path across her collar bone. She throws her head back and lets out the sexiest whimper I have ever heard.

"Fuck baby, I am trying so hard to control myself, but I have wanted you for too long," I tell her as I walk over to the bed and throw her down on it. She reaches for the hem of her shirt and pulls it up and over her head. Her thick breasts practically spilling out of her black bra has me nearly finishing on the spot. I must grab my length through my pants and squeeze hard to calm myself. She reaches for the hem of her pants and pulls them down her long tan legs. I watch the show she is putting on for me and see that she is not wearing panties. I see her soft pink lips and cannot control myself anymore. I dive onto the bed, fitting my shoulders between her legs and spreading her open in front of me. I groan as I see her wetness leaking out and onto the bed.

I use my fingers to spread her open and then lick one long swipe up her entrance, all the way to her bundle of nerves. She lets out a loud moan and she bucks her hips, trying to get the contact she needs to orgasm. I dive back in and eat her like a man starved. After a few minutes of torturing her by taking her to the edge and then backing off, she finally begs me to let her come. I attach my lips to her clit, insert a finger inside of her and then suck hard. Her back bows off the bed and she grabs a fist full of my hair as she rides out her pleasure.

Jo pushes my head off her when she becomes too sensitive, so I look up at her and she has never looked so beautiful to me. Her cheeks are flushed, and her eyes are open wide. I crawl my way up her body, kissing her lips as I position myself at her entrance. I make eye contact with her for my next words.

"I am clean baby. I don't want anything between us. I want to be able to feel all of you."

Jo moans at my words and then looks embarrassed. I pull back a little to see her face, confused on why she would be embarrassed right now after what we just did.

"I am clean too considering I have never been with anyone. Like at all," she says quietly.

I let out a moan as the rest of the blood in my body rushes to my dick. I rest my head on her shoulder and kiss my way to her ear.

"You have no idea how much this means to me Princess. That I get to be your first and your last. I love you, Jo," I utter the words I have wanted to say since the first time I laid eyes on her.

"I love you too, Derrick. Now please make me yours," she begs as she lifts her hips to mine. I position myself at her entrance again and then slowly inch my way inside of her, rocking back and forth. She is so tight that for a second I am afraid she might squeeze my cock too much and we will be done before we even start. I keep rocking back and forth until I am buried to the hilt inside of her. I pause and look at her, memorizing this moment.

After a few seconds of this, Jo moves her hips and I pull myself backwards slowly. We both moan at the sensation.

"I want to take it slow for your first time, but I am hanging on by a thread Princess," I groan as I push my way back inside of her tight channel.

"I don't want you to hold back Derrick. I want all of you," she says and my last thread of restraint snaps. I start thrusting my hips, my cock dragging in and out of her. The headboard starts banging on the wall and I know we are being loud, but I couldn't give a flying fuck right now. I feel my orgasm start at the base of my spine, but I slow down so I can make sure Jo finishes first. I reach down between us and use my thumb to apply pressure and rub little circles on her clit. Her channel tightens on my cock, and she throws her head back as she orgasms. The squeezing sensation is enough to make me explode so I plant myself as deep as I can go and let out a long groan as I release my seed into her warmth.

I collapse on top of her but put my weight on my arms, so I don't crush her. I kiss her and then lay my forehead against hers.

"I love you Derrick," she whispers as she tightens her channel around my cock again. I groan.

"I love you too, Princess. You keep doing that and we are going to be going again right now."

"Maybe that is what I want," she says. We end up making love all night, until the first sunlight comes through the window. We finally fall asleep wrapped up in each other and I couldn't imagine my life any other way with any other woman.

Chapter Twenty-One

Decisions Determine Destiny

Demon

I wake to the sound of someone pounding on my door. I jump out of bed, startling Jo awake. She rubs the sleep out of her eyes, and I stop to stare at her for a second. Damn, she is so beautiful, and I am so screwed.

"What is going on?" she asks, and I remember the pounding that woke me up in the first place.

"I don't know baby, hold on," I say as I stride to the door. I stop when Jo calls my name and turn to look at her. Her eyes drift downwards, and I follow, realizing that I am completely naked, so I grab a pair of boxers and slide them on. I open the door to find Viper standing there, covered in blood.

"What the fuck?" I ask loudly.

"The paramedics just came and took Violet. I came home to find her in the bathtub. She had cut her wrists," he says, staring at his bloody hands. Jo must have heard him because she jumps out of bed, still named, so I tell her to get dressed first and step into the hallway, closing the door.

"What happened?" I ask him.

He shakes his head and says, "I don't know. I came home and found her like that. The only thing she said was that she was so sorry repeatedly."

"Where have you been?" I ask him.

He just looks away in embarrassment, so I stand there and cross my arms, waiting for him to answer me.

"The strip club, alright? I needed a fucking break man. She won't talk to me, and I couldn't take it anymore. I went to get a drink at the strip club so I could have a minute to breathe," he growls. The door to my bedroom is ripped open and a crying Jo comes out, storming right up to Viper and pokes him in the chest.

"You are pathetic. My best friend goes through being raped and losing her child and YOU needed a break? How do you think she felt when you left? You knew she was having trouble coping with all of this and yet you decided going to a strip club was more important?" she yells at him. I see Viper's face transform into anger, so I go to grab Jo, but she holds up her hand to stop me.

"You don't get to judge me. Where were you? Too busy fucking the President huh?" Viper snaps at Jo and I lunge into action. I grab Viper by the shirt and throw him against the wall, pinning him with my arm on his neck.

"You will watch your fucking mouth when you talk to my Old Lady, got it?" I seethe. Jo comes up behind me and places her hand on my back. I relax against her but keep my hold on Viper.

"It's fine Derrick," she says to me before directing her attention back to Viper. "It wasn't my child she lost. It wasn't my club that got her kidnapped. It wasn't me who she was in love with Viper. It was you. She needed you."

Viper's face pales as he takes in what Jo has said.

"Oh shit, what have I done?" he whispers. I let him go and step back, letting Jo handle this situation.

"You need to go be there for her Viper. Go sit at her bedside and just be her rock. She is going to need you now more than ever," Jo tells him.

Viper nods his head and thanks Jo before rushing down the hall. I yell after him, "Take a shower first. You look like you just came out of a horror movie." He throws a thumbs up and changes direction to his room. I turn to Jo, taking her into my arms and pressing a kiss to the top of her head.

"You make an excellent President's Old Lady," I tell her.

"You think so?" she asks.

"Princess, you handled that situation like a boss," I tell her as I lead her back into our bedroom. We undress again and get back into bed. She throws a leg over mine, an arm across my stomach and lays her head on my chest. We stay up for a while to talk about what we expect for our future. At around noon, my phone rings and when I see Viper's name pop up, I hit answer putting it on speaker so Jo can hear about Violet.

"Hey Viper. Is Violet, okay?" I ask. The line is silent for a second before the voice that haunts my woman's nightmares comes over the speaker.

"I don't know about Violet, but Viper here doesn't look too good," Trent laughs into the phone.

"What the fuck do you want Trent? Where is Viper?" I growl into the phone. I look over at Jo and see that her face is completely pale, and she looks ready to vomit.

"Viper is a little," a pause, "tied up at the moment." Trent laughs at his own joke. "As for what I want. I want my property and men that you stole from me, again. Jo and my men for Viper."

THE END… for now.

Acknowledgments

If you had told me just a few months ago that I would be publishing this book, I would have thought you were crazy. It took me a long time to get the courage to sit down and spend my time on writing a book that I was passionate about. I fell in love with these characters as I envisioned this story in my head.

I want to thank every single person who believed in me while I was writing this. Thank you to anyone who told me I could do this and stuck by my side through the entire process, even when I was crabby and stressed.

This has been such a journey for me to be on and I plan on writing this entire series within the next year. I know that sounds like a lot, but this is something I love to do.

I want to thank the people who took the time to read this book and who will take the time to read my next books. If it wasn't for the readers, authors would be nowhere.

Made in the USA
Las Vegas, NV
26 December 2022